Table of Contents

Rourke
Educational Media
rourkeeducationalmedia.com

Can you find these words?

gifts

parade

pie

pumpkins

What is a Holiday?

Holidays are special days.

Holidays only come once a year.

They are days of celebration.

Christmas is a holiday.

gift

People give **gifts.**
They sing special songs.

Some people like to decorate for holidays.

pumpkins

Pumpkins and bats for Halloween!

Some people eat special foods.

Pumpkin **pie** for Thanksgiving!

pie

Some holidays have a **parade.**

parade

How do you spend your holidays?

Did you find these words?

People give **gifts**.

Some holidays have a **parade**.

Pumpkin **pie** for Thanksgiving!

Pumpkins and bats for Halloween!

Photo Glossary

 **gifts** (gifts): Presents, or things you give to someone for a special day.

 **parade** (puh-RADE): A festive line of people and vehicles that are part of a holiday or festivity.

 **pie** (pye): A pastry filled with fruit, custard, meat, or vegetables and baked in an oven.

 **pumpkins** (PUHMP-kins): Big, round, orange squash with thick rinds and many seeds.

Index

About the Author

Michelle Garcia Andersen loves to celebrate lots of holidays. Her favorite holiday is Christmas. She loves the decorations, the delicious food, and spending the day with her family.

www.rourkeeducationalmedia.com

PHOTO CREDITS: Cover ©evgenyatamanenko, Page 3 ©fstop123, Page 4-5 ©By India Picture, Page 2,6-7,14,15 ©eli_asenova, Page 2,8-9,14,15 ©Roman Samborskyi, Page 2,10-11,14,15 ©YinYang, Page 2,12-13,14,15 ©jcarillet

Edited by: Keli Sipperley
Cover design by: Kathy Walsh
Interior design by: Rhea Magaro-Wallace

Library of Congress PCN Data
What is a Holiday? / Michelle Garcia Andersen
(Discovery Days)
ISBN (hard cover)(alk. paper) 978-1-64156-181-5
ISBN (soft cover) 978-1-64156-237-9
ISBN (e-Book) 978-1-64156-289-8
Library of Congress Control Number: 2017957790

Printed in the United States of America, North Mankato, Minnesota